Paul and
Sandra 2

Paul and Sandra 2

Peter Leigh

Published in association with
The Basic Skills Agency

Hodder & Stoughton
A MEMBER OF THE HODDER HEADLINE GROUP

Orders: please contact Bookpoint Ltd, 39 Milton Park, Abingdon, Oxon
OX14 4TD. Telephone: (44) 01235 400414, Fax: (44) 01235 400454. Lines are
open from 9.00 - 6.00, Monday to Saturday, with a 24 hour message answering
service. Email address: orders@bookpoint.co.uk

British Library Cataloguing in Publication Data
A catalogue record for this title is available from The British Library

ISBN 0 340 73818 9

First published 1995
Impression number 10 9 8 7 6 5 4 3 2 1
Year   2004 2003 2002 2001 2000 1999 1998

Typeset by Transet Limited, Coventry, England.
Printed in Great Britain for Hodder & Stoughton Educational, a division of
Hodder Headline Plc, 338 Euston Road, London, NW1 3BH by
Athenaeum Press Ltd, Gateshead, Tyne & Wear.

1

....

'She's not coming,' said Johnny.
Paul said nothing. There was a long silence.
'She's not coming.' Paul still said nothing.
'I said she's no...'

'I heard what you said,' said Paul, 'and I
don't want to hear any more.'

They were sitting in a pub in Portonsea.
Sandra had said she would see him in the pub
at eight o'clock. It was now nine o'clock.

'No,' said Johnny. 'She's not coming!.. Not
now!.. No chance!.. Women!.. Typical!.. You
can't trust...'

'Look, will you just shut up! I told you.
I don't want to hear it.'

'Well, I'm just trying to talk to you.
We are having a drink together.
We are meant to be friends.
And let me tell you, it's not easy at

the moment. You've had your
eyes fixed on that door ever since
we got here.'

'I don't want to miss her, that's all.'

'Miss her? Miss her? You won't miss her.
She's missed you! She's missed you,
and gone off with someone else.'

'She might have been held up.'

'Held up? Stop kidding yourself. She
hasn't been held up – you've been
stood up!'

Paul looked away. He felt as if there
was a big stone in his stomach.
'Let's give her ten more minutes.'

'Ten more minutes? Ten more minutes
sitting here? Listen Paul, while we are
sitting inside here, outside there are girls,
hundreds of them, and they are all
desperate. They are all desperate for me.
They are just itching to get their hands
on me. They are aching for my body.
And what am I doing? Sitting here with you.'

'That's all it is with you, isn't it?
Sex! Sex! Sex!'

'That's right!'

'No romance!'

'No!'

'No finer feelings.'

'No!'

'Just "Come here, darling", and wham,
bam, bam!'

'That's right! And let me tell you, they love it.
They can't get enough of it.'

'Rubbish! Sandra's not like that.'

'They're all like that!'

'Listen, I feel sorry for the girls that go
with you. They're desperate all right,
but not in the way you mean.'

'Well, at least they don't say they'll meet
me at eight o'clock, and then stand me up!'

Paul looked away again. 'I tell you, she's been held up.' But he didn't really believe it.

'Oh yes, well we've heard that one before, haven't we? And besides Mr Pure-and-holy, what about you?'

'What do you mean, what about me?'

'I saw you with Sandra this morning. I saw the look on your face. I know what you were thinking, and it wasn't all sweetness and light.'

'Well, of course not, but that's different.'

'No it's not! It's not different at all. It's exactly the same.'

'No it's not! You make it all sound dirty.'

'Well that's how I like it, the dirtier the better.'

Paul groaned. 'There's no talking to you.'

'Look,' said Johnny. 'All I'm saying is that men and women, boys and girls, blokes and birds, they're all just the same.

They're no different. They all want just one thing, and one thing only. And all the rest is moonshine.'

'I don't just want one thing and one thing only.'

'What do you want then?'

'Hundreds of things, thousands of things, and all of them different...' Paul's voice trailed off. 'Well, I don't know exactly what I do want, but I do know there's more in it than what you're saying.'

'Like what?'

'Well, like when I was talking to Sandra this morning. It was only about ten minutes, but it was great. We could have gone on forever. It was so exciting.'

'Oh yes?'

'Yes, exciting!'

'I know what was exciting you.'

'It wasn't like that at all. I wanted to tell
her things. It was as if she really knew
me, really understood me.'

'It must be love.'

'And when she looked at me with
those eyes...'

'Listen,' said Johnny suddenly, and he
clutched Paul's arm. 'Listen, can you hear
them?' He cupped his hand round his ear.
'Quiet! Listen! Yes! Ding-dong, ding-dong!
The sound of wedding bells! Ding-dong,
ding-dong. I can hear them clearly.'

Paul shook himself free. 'Get off,
you daft idiot.'

'No I'm serious. You start off thinking like
that, and that's how you'll end up.
A life sentence. A ball and chain
round your neck from now until whenever.
And who are you calling an idiot?
At least I don't go all lovey-dovey
over a girl I've only met for ten minutes,
and who stood me up on our very first date.'

'It wasn't exactly a date. She just said she'd be in here with her friends.'

'Well, she's not here is she? With or without her friends. She...' But he broke off, staring over Paul's shoulder.

Paul spun round. There was Sandra.

2

......

She was standing in the doorway.
She was wearing a tee-shirt and jeans.
Paul felt his heart jump.

She looked worried. Paul went straight
across to her. She smiled when she saw him.
'Oh thank goodness you're still here.
I thought you might have gone.
You might have thought I wasn't coming.'

'No, of course not!' Paul didn't say that
was exactly what he had been thinking,
that she wasn't coming, that she had
stood him up. But he didn't say those things
because they didn't matter anymore.
She was here. That was all that mattered, and
now everything was all right again.

There were some friends following
her through the door, Kate and Lisa,
Gary and Richard, but Paul didn't catch
all the names. He was too busy
looking at Sandra. She was saying that
there had been trouble with the car,
and that was why they were late, but Paul

didn't care. She could have been ten
hours late, and he still wouldn't have cared.
She was there. That was enough.

Everyone was laughing and talking
and getting themselves drinks. Soon
Johnny was entertaining them all with stories
of his motorbike. Paul sat next to Sandra.
No-one paid them much attention.

Sandra said, 'I was really worried in case
you had gone. And what you would
think of me.'

Paul said, 'I know what I think of you.'

Sandra blushed. 'Anyway,' she said, 'what
were you and Johnny saying as I came in?'
Paul looked blank. 'I thought you were
having an argument.'

'Oh that.' It seemed so long ago now that Paul
had to think hard. 'It was nothing really.'

'Nothing?'

'No... well, if you must know, we were
arguing about girls.'

'Girls?'

'Yes, Johnny was saying that they're
just the same as boys. All after the
same thing.'

'And what's that?'

'Oh, you know... sex!'

'Oh, I see... and what do you think?'

'Me?'

'Do you think all girls are after the same
thing as all boys?'

'I don't know. How would I know? But then
I don't think that all boys are out for
the same thing in any case.'

'What about Johnny?'

'Oh Johnny... well, the thing about Johnny is
that he wants everyone to think he's really
tough. He says all these things just to make
people think he's cool and hard, as though he
doesn't give a damn about anything.'

12

'All boys do that.'

'Do they?'

'Well, most... they come up to you and say
the stupidest things, as if they're so tough,
as if you're meant to be impressed.
And girls don't care about things like that.
I don't care how tough a boy is, it's
underneath that matters.'

'That's it with Johnny. That's exactly it,
because underneath he's not like
that at all. Underneath he's as soft as
anything, but he doesn't want
anyone to know.'

'And what about you?'

'Me?'

'Yes, are you as soft as anything underneath?'

Paul laughed. 'Well, you'll just have to find
out for yourself.'

'And how am I going to do that?'

'You'll just have to get to know me really well, just like I know you.'

'What? You don't know me at all.'

'Yes I do. I know all about you.'

'What do you know about me?'

'Well, I know your name's Sandra...'

'Everyone knows that.'

'...and I know you work in a chemist's...'

'How amazing! What a detective!'

'...and I know you like pickled onions with honey.'

'Pickled onions with honey? What makes you think I like that?'

'All beautiful girls like pickled onions with honey. Didn't you know that? It's a well-known fact.'

Sandra laughed. 'What a line! What a smoothie! Where did you pick that one up? From your grandad?'

'No, I made it up just now. Doesn't stop it being true though.'

'You've been watching too much tele. You know, all the romantic adverts, where he gives her boxes of chocolates.'

'Well, I haven't got any chocolates – how about half of shandy?'

'What an offer! How can a girl refuse? Tell you what, throw in a packet of crisps as well.'

'You're on. Plain ones?'

'Plain ones? Plain ones? Where do you think you are? This is Portonsea. This is a classy place. Cheese and onion or nothing.'

3

......

Paul felt so good. He could have been drunk, except he had not had much to drink. It was just sitting with Sandra, being with her and talking to her.

When he had bought the drinks, she told him more about herself. She was only working at the chemist's for the present. She might go to college, but what she really wanted to do was travel. She had been born in Portonsea, and lived there all her life, but now she wanted to get away.

'I mean I like Portonsea,' she said, 'and I've got lots of friends here, but it's just the same thing day after day, week after week. I want to be free. I want to see something of the world. Somewhere different, where the people are different, where the air is different.'

'The moon over Kashmir, sunset on the Pacific.'

'That's right, although sometimes I think just a day trip to France would be enough.'

Paul laughed. 'Yes I know. All my friends go on about a career, or just getting a job these days, but I keep thinking there must be something more – there must be something more in life than just working for a pension.'

'Well, what about me? All my friends keep talking about getting married and settling down. I haven't done anything to settle down from. I mean, can you imagine me married?'

Paul didn't say anything. He didn't like to say what he was imagining about Sandra.

'What about your Mum and Dad?' he asked. 'What do they say about you going off round the world?'

'I just live with my Mum. She says "Go while you can." She would if she had the chance.'

'And what about...' Paul held his breath, '...your boyfriend?'

Sandra turned and smiled at him.

'What boyfriend is that then?'

Paul was embarrassed. 'Well, I don't know, I was just asking.'

'And what about you? Won't there be any girl to miss you if you go off round the world?'

'Chance would be a fine thing. No, there won't. No-one at all. At least not until now.'

'Why?' Sandra looked at him, her eyes wide and clear. 'What's different about now?'

Paul gulped. 'Well... well...'

'Hey, you two lovebirds!' It was Johnny. Sandra grinned, and Paul blushed. 'Sorry to break up such a cosy little chat, but we're all going to the fair. Are you coming?'

Sandra jumped up. 'Of course we're coming.' But Paul sat still. He hated fairs. The rides made him feel sick, and the lights gave him a headache.

'Well... er...' he said, but Sandra reached over and grabbed his hand.
'Come on Paul!' she said, and she didn't let go.

4

Afterwards Paul didn't know whether
it was the night, the drink, or Sandra
herself who made it all so wonderful.

He had never enjoyed a fair like it.
They went on the waltzers, the big
wheel, and the dodgems. Each ride
was more exciting than the last. He
won a locket for her on the rifle range –
'I'll wear it forever,' she said – and she
squealed and clung to him on the ghost train.
She had her fortune told – 'You have
just met a handsome stranger!' – and they
ate hot dogs with candy floss. It was
everything a fair was meant to be.

Paul didn't know how long they had been
there when Johnny appeared in front of them.
'Everyone's going,' he said. 'I'm giving Kate
a lift.'

'We'll be all right,' said Paul. Johnny looked
at them both. He smiled, and went off.

'I'll have to go home,' said Sandra.

21

'I'll take you home,' said Paul.

'What about you?'

'Don't worry about me. I'll be all right.'

Sandra laughed. 'Let's go by the sea.'

The fair was by the beach. They walked
down to the shore. The lights were behind
them, and in front of them was the night
and the sea. It was cool. They stood
by the edge of the waves. They could see
the reflection of the moon and the stars.

'I love it down here,' said Sandra. 'I come here
all the time when there aren't any people
around.'

They stood very close, very still. He leaned
towards her. Gently their heads touched.
She didn't move away. A wisp of her hair
blew across and touched his face.
He turned towards her, and she shifted
closer to him. His lips brushed across
her cheek. It was damp from the sea
spray. He tasted salt. 'Oh Sandra,'
he said, and pulled her to him. She turned
fully, leant back, and kissed him.

'I've got to go home,' she whispered. But he
wanted more. More of her lips, her hair,
her lovely slimness. He wouldn't let her go.
And again she kissed him.

'I've got to go,' she said.

'Kiss me again,' he said, but she twisted
out of his arms laughing.

'You'll have to catch me first,' she said,
and was off. She sprinted across the sands
with Paul after her. And every dip and hollow
and every pool, became the excuse
for a chase and a capture and a surrender.

'Listen,' said Sandra, and she put her hand
over his mouth. 'Listen, I've got to go home.'
By now they were in the street where she
lived. 'It's not far, but my mum will be
worried about me.'

'Oh... oh yes, of course.'

'What about you? How will you get home?
Back to your tent?'

'Don't worry. I'll be all right. I'll walk
back easy. But... but...'

'But what?' They were outside Sandra's house now.

'But... shall I see you again?'

'Of course you shall. If you want to that is.' She looked up at him shyly.

'Want to? Of course I want to! I don't want anything else. Listen Sandra,' he said, and pulled her close again. 'You're like no-one else I've ever met. You're lovely, you're...'

'Goodnight Sandra!' said a voice at his elbow. Sandra broke away.

'Oh! Goodnight Mrs Hudson. Goodnight Mr Hudson.' A middle-aged couple walked by. 'Neighbours,' she whispered. 'I must go now.'

'Oh Sandra.'

'Listen. Come tomorrow afternoon, about two. But I must go now. Goodnight.'

'Tomorrow afternoon. Of course. But Sandra...'

'I must go.'

'Sandra...'

'Goodnight.'

'I love you.'

But she was gone.

If you have enjoyed reading this book, you may be interested in other titles in the *Livewire* series.

The following exciting **Youth Fiction** stories are currently available: